Little SHARK

Little SHARK

Anne Rockwell

Pictures by Megan Halsey

Walker & Company ✹ New York

First published in the United States of America in 2005 by
Walker Publishing Company, Inc.

Published simultaneously in Canada by Fitzhenry and Whiteside,
Markham, Ontario L3R 4T8

For information about permission to reproduce selections from
this book, write to Permissions, Walker & Company,
104 Fifth Avenue, New York, New York 10011

Library of Congress Cataloging-in-Publication Data

Rockwell, Anne F.
Little shark / Anne Rockwell ; pictures by Megan Halsey.
      p. cm.
ISBN 0-8027-8955-2 (hc) — ISBN 0-8027-8956-0 (re)
1. Sharks—Juvenile literature. I. Halsey, Megan, ill. II. Title.

QL638.9.R64 2005
597.3—dc22
                                    2004052611

The artwork for this book was created with
watercolors and colored pencils on water-
color paper and bristol. The backgrounds
were painted with watercolors on gessoed
illustration board.

The artist would like to thank Peter Noah
for his assistance.

Book design by Nicole Gastonguay

Visit Walker & Company's Web site at
www.walkeryoungreaders.com

Printed in Hong Kong

10 9 8 7 6 5 4 3 2 1

For Christian & Tudy
—A.R.
For Steve & Tim &
Miss Renee & Marty
—M.H.

In the dark deepness of the sea

Little Shark is born,

along with his forty-nine brothers and sisters.

He's not very big—only about ten inches long.

The huge mother shark swims away

as soon as all her little sharks are born.

So do Little Shark's forty-nine brothers and sisters.

Little Shark is all alone,

on his own in the deep and dangerous sea.

Swim fast, Little Shark!

This enormous sea is full of hungry sharks
that are much bigger than you.
They have plenty of sharp teeth
to gobble up smaller fish—even little sharks.

They can't chew,
so they bite off chunks of their
prey with their sharp teeth and gobble
the chunk in one swallow.

Little Shark is hungry, too.

Watch out, all you tiny fish! Swim fast!

Little Shark was born with plenty of sharp teeth.

Most animals have to keep their grown-up teeth

all of their lives.

But sharks can grow new teeth whenever they need to.

Sharks can feel the vibrations fish in danger make when they swim,
even when those fish are far away.

Little Shark keeps swimming and swimming
in the deep darkness of the sea.

He usually stays below where the sunlight can reach.

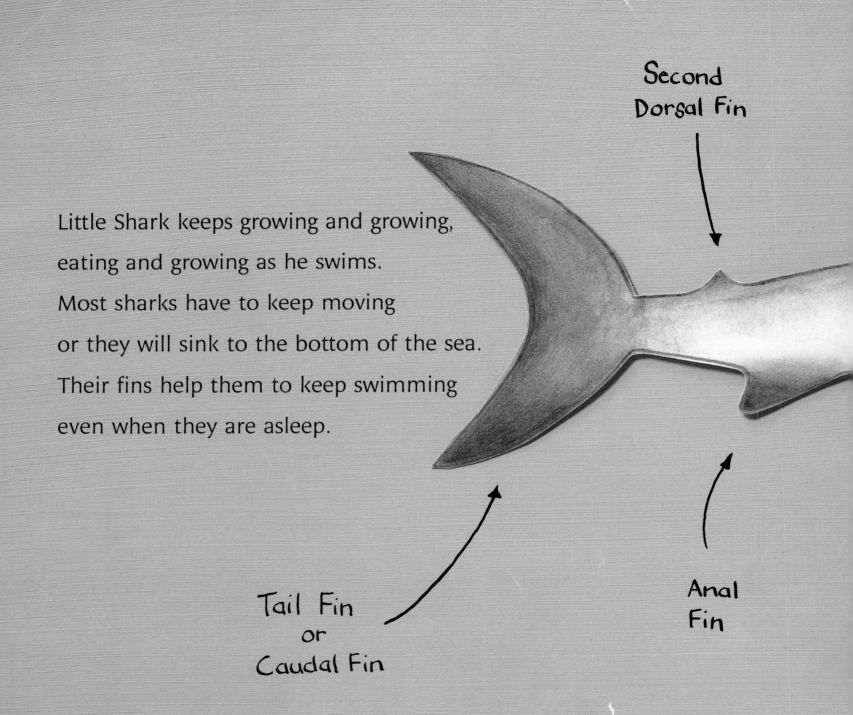

Second
Dorsal Fin

Little Shark keeps growing and growing,
eating and growing as he swims.
Most sharks have to keep moving
or they will sink to the bottom of the sea.
Their fins help them to keep swimming
even when they are asleep.

Tail Fin
or
Caudal Fin

Anal
Fin

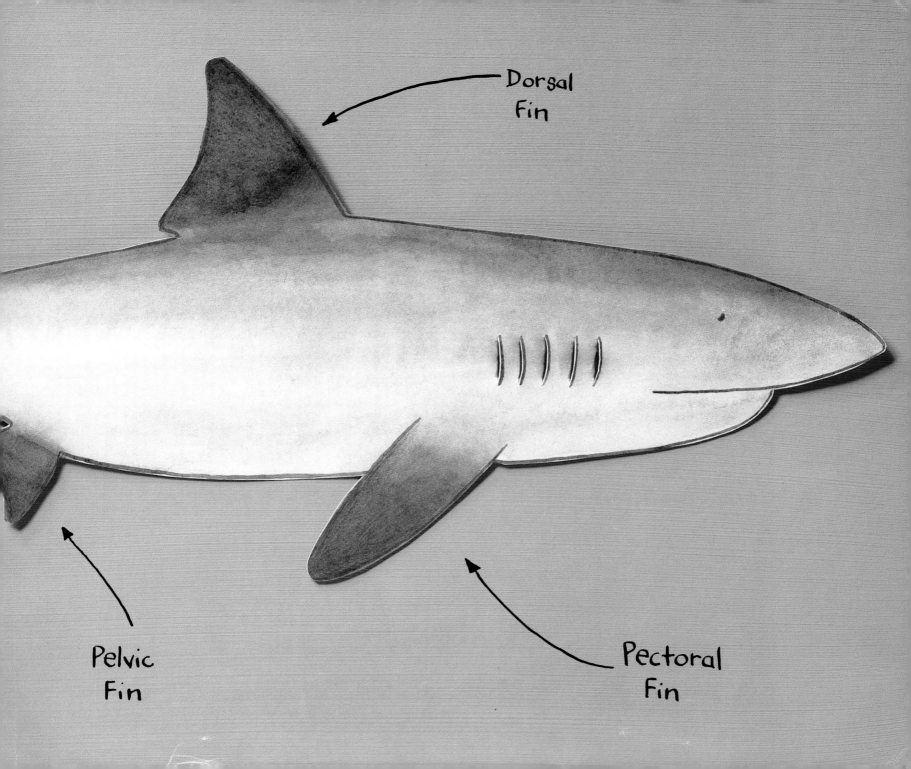

Dorsal
Fin

Pelvic
Fin

Pectoral
Fin

All animals need oxygen to live.
We get it from the air we breathe,
but sharks and other fish get it from
the water they swim in.

Most sharks have to keep swimming so water full of fresh oxygen can pass through their gills.

That's how they breathe.

Codfish Skeleton: Bones

Ribs

Shark Skeleton: Cartilage

Gill Arches

Little Shark's skeleton isn't like the skeleton of other fish.

Other fish have hard bones.

A shark's skeleton is made of rubbery cartilage,

like the tip of your nose, not bones.

A fish's skeleton is like our bones.

Little Shark doesn't have smooth and slippery scales
like other fish.
Sharkskin is covered
with thousands of tiny, curved sharp tips, like a shark's tooth.
Years ago, people used this rough sharkskin instead of sandpaper
to rub wood smooth.

Shark
Denticles

Fish
Scales

Little Shark keeps swimming and eating,
eating and growing.
What kind of shark
do you think Little Shark will grow up to be?

Little Shark has grown into a **big blue shark!**

See—no big shark has caught him.

No fishermen has caught him either.

Little Shark will reach twelve to thirteen feet long,

as he keeps growing until he is old.

He will keep growing as he swims

all around the world.

Author's Note

Sharks are some of the most ancient animals living today. Four hundred thousand years ago, there were sharks similar to those that live today in the sea.

There are many different kinds of sharks, but I chose to make Little Shark in this story grow up to be a blue shark. They are beautiful, with their long, sleek bodies, blue on the back, fading to white underneath (although the intense blue color they are while alive quickly fades to blue-gray after they are caught).

Blue sharks are believed to be the fastest-swimming fish in the sea and are found world-wide. No one knows exactly how fast they swim, but scientists think their speed is between thirty-five and sixty miles an hour.

A female blue shark is able to give birth to pups by the time she is about five years old. She can have anywhere from twenty to over a hundred pups, but she usually gives birth to more as she gets older and bigger. Blue sharks live to be about twenty years old. Like many fish, they keep growing all their lives and can grow up to thirteen feet in length.

Blue sharks are predators, which means they eat other animals. Their favorite food is squid. Although they have hurt fewer people than many other animals, all the same, we should always be on the lookout for shark fins when we go to the beach and avoid swimming at night or in murky water. But human beings are the most dangerous enemies sharks have. Fisherman catch them on lines for sport, and they are often caught accidentally in the wide nets set out to catch schools of smaller fish.

If you're curious about these remarkably interesting animals, you can visit an aquarium, a safe place for people and sharks to observe one another.